DEDICATION

We dedicate this book to all young people
who struggle with sad and anxious feelings.

We would like to thank the readers of the Latinx communities
who reviewed, discussed, and contributed to the book you're reading today.

Printed in the United States of America

First Printing, 2019

www.pebblespress.com

ISBN: 978-1-7337582-0-8

info@palomasecret.com

The sun was melting into purple and pink swirls in the clouds while Paloma played with her best friends Yesenia and Marisol in the pool. Mamá and Papá stood nearby and watched.

"Time to go, Paloma!" Mamá shouted.

She knew she couldn't bargain for more time, so she said good-bye and pulled herself up and out of the water.

She wrapped herself up in a towel and hurried over to Mamá and Papá. "Can we go to Icy's, please?"

Mamá's shoulders dropped. "It's late, Paloma. Alicia needs to get to bed, and I have the early shift in the hospital."

Paloma's Secret

Written by
Amy Fabrikant & Mia Hood

Illustrated by
Kenneth López

"Please, Mamá, Alicia's already asleep, and I promise I'll be quick."
Papá rubbed the towel over her head.

"Bueno, vamos," Mamá said as she tucked Alicia's blanket under her.

As they left the Thomas Jefferson Pool,
Paloma slipped her hand into Mamá's
and skipped along beside her.

On days like today, when I wake up, I lift up and up out of bed, and I glide into the morning light. My hair flaps on my back. My arms slip through the air. I leap and land, I rise and rise.

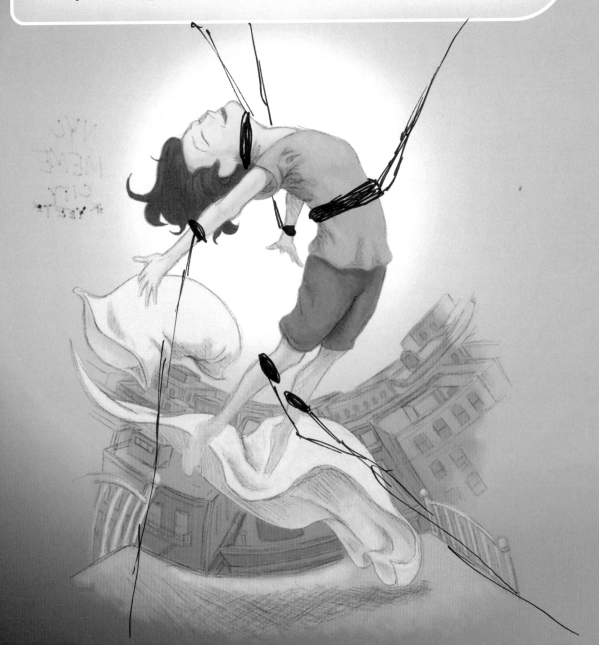

The next morning, Paloma was quick to jump out of bed and put on the skirt and sneakers Mamá had bought for the first day of school. Before long, Marisol and Yesenia arrived, tumbling into the room, chattering about their new classes. Marisol sat cross-legged on her bed to fix Paloma's wavy hair into braids while Yesenia arranged freshly sharpened pencils in her pencil pouch.

Soon enough, Paloma, Marisol, and Yesenia scrambled out of her room. They grabbed tostadas from Papá and took off, arm in arm, for their first day of fifth grade.

Even so, today,
I maybe-kinda think
I feel this tiny tingle
between my toes.

It's a feeling I've felt before.

But how could it be
that I'd feel a tiny tingle,
a little-prickly-itchy-pesky tickle,
when everything else
is perfect and sweet?

"How's school going, Paloma?" Papá asked over dinner one night. "You haven't told us much lately."

Paloma took a sip of water. "Good."

"What did you and Marisol decide for Halloween?" Mamá asked.

"We're going to be a rock band."

"That sounds fun!" Mamá replied.

"Yeah, Yesenia and Marisol are happy about it." Paloma made herself swallow another bite of rice and beans.

"Did you tell Mamá about soccer?" Papá asked.

"Our team is first in the league." Paloma didn't look up from her plate.

I wiggle my toes to make it stop. I curl them up inside my socks. I fan them out and scrunch them up. But it's still there.

And what happens next is slow to happen, but I know it'll happen all the same.

Sweet things start tasting not-sweet. The bright air starts looking not-bright.

Papá fed Alicia a spoonful of applesauce and took out his phone to scroll through his soccer pictures. "Oh, you have to tell Mamá about all the goals you stopped!"

Paloma stood up and went into the kitchen to get more water. As she filled her glass, she closed her eyes and took a breath. The water spilled over the rim of the glass and onto her hand.

"¿Qué te pasa, mi hijita? ," Papá said.

Paloma returned to the table and wiped her wet hand on her lap. She forced a smile. "I'm just tired. I've been thinking about dropping soccer."

Mamá's eyes widened. "Paloma, your team needs you! You can't just sit out because you're tired."

"Sí Mamá," she said and carried her plate to the sink.

By November, the autumn air had turned the treetops golden. On a quiet Monday afternoon, Paloma, Marisol, and Yesenia ate lunch in the school's courtyard. Marisol persuaded their English teacher Ms. Rodríguez to join them.

As Marisol carried on about her winning goal at last week's soccer game, Paloma tore at the edges of a leaf that had fallen at her feet.

"Paloma, are you feeling okay?" Ms. Rodríguez asked.

Paloma shrugged. "I'm really tired. I don't know if I should play goalie for our next game."

"But you're the best goalie in the league!" Yesenia insisted.

Paloma shrugged again.

On days like today, when I wake up,
I feel them creeping up my legs.

And this time, it's not just a tiny tingle,
a mere prickly-itchy-pesky tickle.

They've grown into a twisty,
knotty tangle, locking my legs
from my knees to my ankles.

The next week in science lab, Yesenia and Marisol giggled as they tried to balance a balloon on a scale to find its mass. The balloon floated over to Paloma, bounced on her knee and fell to the ground. Paloma didn't move.

And if I know one thing--
just one little-single-all-by-itself-individual thing--
it's that, today, they are definitely there.

"Paloma!" her teacher shouted. "Pay attention!"

Paloma's stomach tightened as her classmates snickered. Her eyes grew hot.

"Why don't you go to the bathroom and come back ready to learn?"

My books
stacked so neat,
the pleats of my skirt
so sharp and clean.

But seeing is not enough.

If only
I could feel
and smell
and taste
and reach out
to touch the world.

The late afternoon sun broke through the tree branches and lit the soccer field. Paloma stood in the goal, picking at her nails.

Downfield, Marisol passed the ball to Yesenia, and Yesenia leaped into the air and volleyed it into the goal. The team surrounded Yesenia to celebrate their victory. From where Paloma stood, they looked like a cluster of bouncing ponytails.

The world looks so bright.

I want to take a gulp of it,
dance around in it,
snuggle up next to it,
be a part of it.

On days like today, when I wake up,
my belly's wrapped up in vines. I don't want to get up.

I want to give up, so I try to come up with a lie.

Something to say so no one will make me walk out into the day.

"Paloma, you're still in bed?" Mamá shouted. "You're late for school!"

Paloma tucked her head under the covers.
"I don't feel good. I can't go to school today."

Mamá pulled the covers down and slipped her hand onto Paloma's forehead.

"You don't have a temperature. There's nothing wrong. Vamos!"

"No! I can't go. Please don't make me!" Paloma rolled over onto her pillow and began to cry.

"Fine, but no TV and no iPad!"

As the vines have
grown up and around me,
a fear has grown inside me...

What if these vines that envelope me,
now all the way up to my neck...

What if they start to feel like my home?

What if I belong in them?

What If I belong to them?

And what if they belong to me?

They've taken my shape. Or have I taken theirs?

Maybe this is my home now.

Maybe I'll never be free.

The next morning, Mamá left for work early.

Papá couldn't get Paloma out of bed.

And what if I secretly want to be stuck?

Truly-secretly-desperately love being stuck?

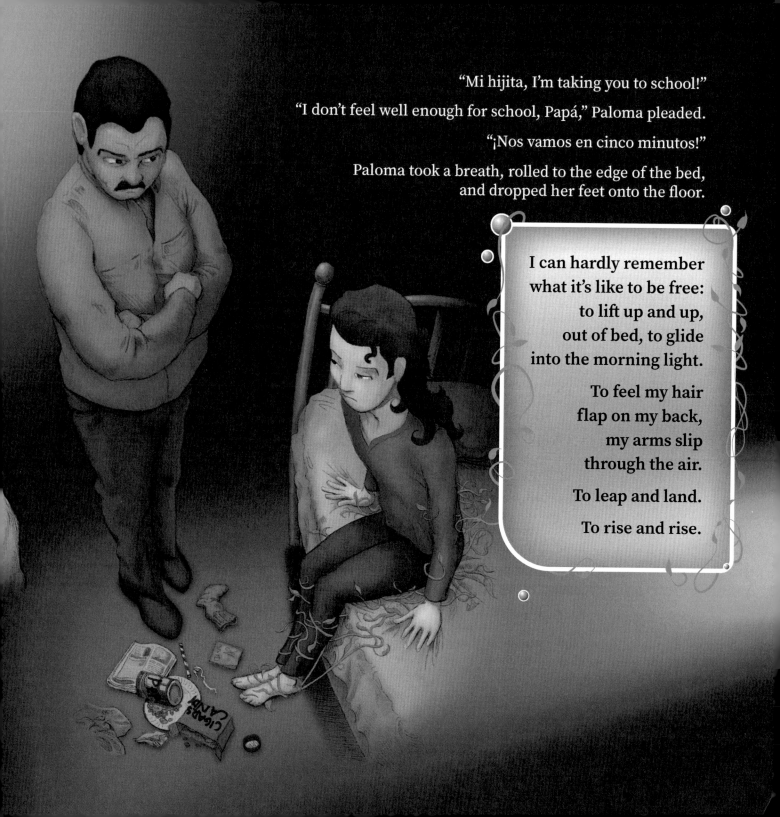

"Mi hijita, I'm taking you to school!"

"I don't feel well enough for school, Papá," Paloma pleaded.

"¡Nos vamos en cinco minutos!"

Paloma took a breath, rolled to the edge of the bed,
and dropped her feet onto the floor.

I can hardly remember
what it's like to be free:
to lift up and up,
out of bed, to glide
into the morning light.

To feel my hair
flap on my back,
my arms slip
through the air.

To leap and land.

To rise and rise.

Paloma was late to English class. At Ms. Rodríguez's door, she pressed her face into the opening and watched Yesenia and Marisol work together. Yesenia showed Marisol a page from her book, and Marisol giggled. The room was buzzing with activity.

Marisol spotted Paloma in the doorway, waved, and motioned for her to come in.

She slunk into the classroom and took her seat next to her friends.

On days like today,
when I wake up,
I know for sure
I'm definitely stuck.

My toes, my knees,
my hips, my belly,
and all the way up
to my neck.

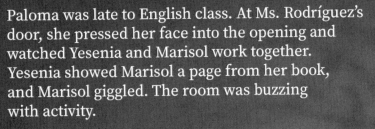

And now these vines have
sprouted leaves—
tiny-little-pointy-jagged leaves—
and buds and little nubs
and a knot of weeds.

Paloma barely looked up
when Ms. Rodríguez leaned down
to welcome her to class.

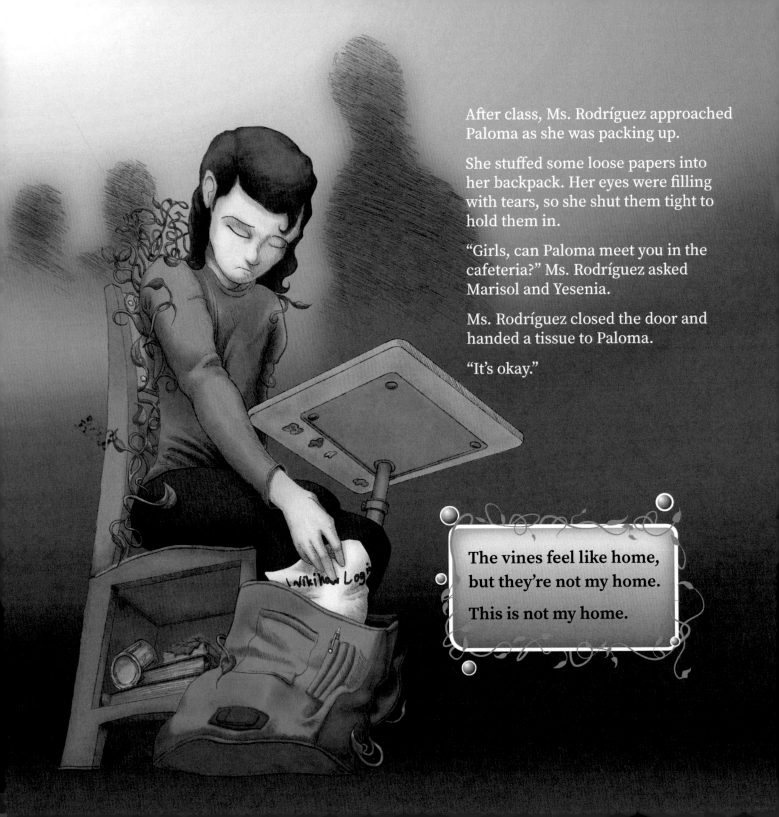

After class, Ms. Rodríguez approached Paloma as she was packing up.

She stuffed some loose papers into her backpack. Her eyes were filling with tears, so she shut them tight to hold them in.

"Girls, can Paloma meet you in the cafeteria?" Ms. Rodríguez asked Marisol and Yesenia.

Ms. Rodríguez closed the door and handed a tissue to Paloma.

"It's okay."

The vines feel like home, but they're not my home.

This is not my home.

"Do you want to tell me what you're feeling?" Ms. Rodríguez asked in a soft voice.

"I-I-I'm scared I'm not normal. Everyone at the soccer game was so excited. And everyone in class today was working together. And all I can do is sit here."

"Have you talked to anyone else about this?"

"I've told my parents that I don't want to go to school, but they just want me to try harder. In the morning, it's like every bone in my body is broken, but nobody knows except me."

"I think I understand, Paloma. I know I've felt that way. It can be hard to describe this feeling to others."

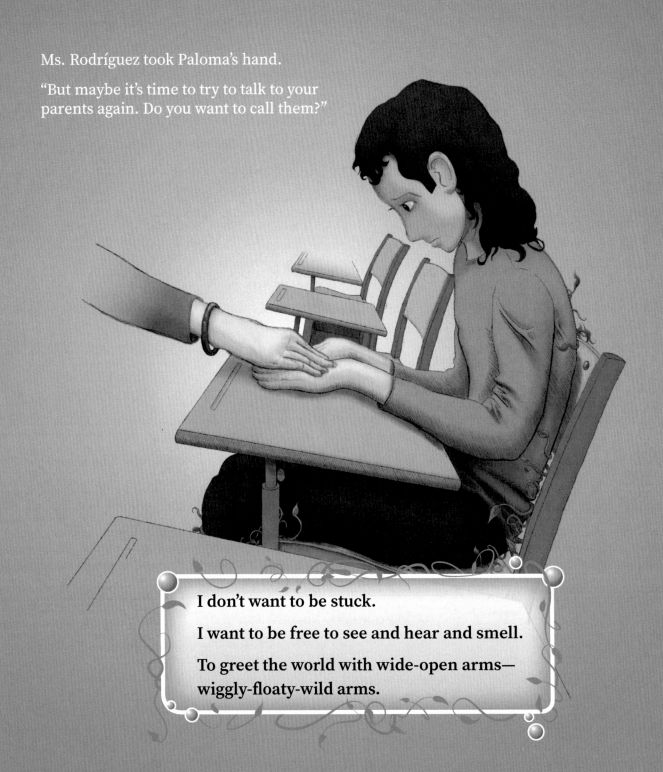

Ms. Rodríguez took Paloma's hand.

"But maybe it's time to try to talk to your parents again. Do you want to call them?"

I don't want to be stuck.

I want to be free to see and hear and smell.

To greet the world with wide-open arms—
wiggly-floaty-wild arms.

Ms. Rodríguez walked Paloma to the nurse's office.

"Why don't you rest here for a bit? I'm going to call your parents, and we can talk to them together."

Paloma lay down on the cot in the corner of the office. She pulled her knees up under her chin and listened to herself breathe.

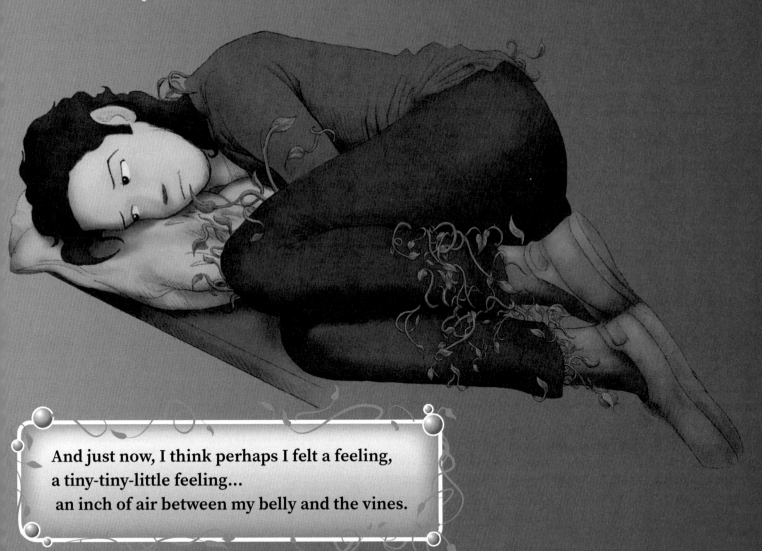

And just now, I think perhaps I felt a feeling,
a tiny-tiny-little feeling...
 an inch of air between my belly and the vines.

Paloma awoke to Mamá stroking her shoulder.

She blinked away the sleep.

"I'm sorry I made you leave work early again."

"It's okay, mi hijita."

Mamá and Papá knelt by Paloma. Papá held her hand.

Ms. Rodríguez and Ms. Joans, the school councilor,
joined them by the cot. Paloma sat up.

"Let's talk about what you've been feeling, Paloma.
It might be depression."

"Ay, Paloma." Mamá hugged her tight. "We're sorry we didn't know what was happening. Why didn't you tell us?"

"I should have, but I felt so scared because I could tell you were mad at me."

"We weren't mad at you. Te amamos," Mamá whispered, holding Paloma close. "We just didn't understand what was going on."

Ms. Joans recommended some names of doctors and therapists for Paloma.

The January sky
was bright white.
The streets below
glistened.

Paloma sat up in bed,
imagining how the cold
winter air would feel
on her cheeks.

"How are the
vines this morning,
Paloma?" Papá asked.

Paloma and Alicia
sat on the bed
playing peek-a-boo.

"They're not too bad,"
Paloma said.

Alicia climbed on top of Paloma and smushed her face into hers.
Everyone laughed.

"Are you sure you feel ready for school?"
Mamá asked.

Mamá gave Paloma a hug
just as the doorbell rang.

It was Marisol.

Paloma gathered her books.

"I'm ready."

Today, when I woke up,
I squirmed and jiggled
and wriggled around.

I made my belly big with air
and blew it out all at once.

I told the vines to loosen up,
to let me wag a finger or a toe,
to shimmy my shoulders
and rock my hips,
to skip and leap and go!

AUTHOR'S NOTE
by Amy Fabrikant

Dear Reader,

According to the National Association of Mental Illness, self-harm, many times a result of depression and anxiety, is the leading cause of death among young people ten and older.

When I was in middle school over thirty years ago, I experienced feelings of loneliness and fear, which I now realize was an expression of my anxiety and depression. I couldn't find my experiences or loneliness depicted in any book, which added to my feelings of alienation and despair. I began to imagine the impact that a book like Paloma's Secret might have for children going through these emotions. My hope is that this book can become a springboard for conversations about our difficult feelings that many times are held in secret.

Feelings of depression and anxiety don't discriminate against any race, ethnicity or culture. My experience as a white educator working across diverse communities has changed the book I imagined writing as a teenager. I recognize now one way that racism has been institutionalized in our country is by the exclusion of positive images and narratives of people of color in our cultural products - like in our children's books. With this in mind, Mia, Kenneth and I worked closely with people of LatinX heritage to tell a story that offers a positive representation of a Mexican American Family.

In this story about Paloma and her secret, her parents become role models for how to be responsive and supportive of the young people in our care; they help to normalize Paloma's experience in a way that empowers her to meet the social and emotional challenges of school life that many of our students experience.

I hope you receive Paloma's Secret with all the love we intended.

www.amyfabrikant.com

CHART OF NEEDS AND FEELINGS

NEEDS

PHYSICAL
BASIC NEEDS FOR REST, SAFETY, FOOD, SHELTER, RELAXATION

CONNECTION
EMPATHY, UNDERSTANDING, TRUST, LOVE, INTIMACY, SHARED REALITY, TO BE SEEN AND HEARD

PLAY
FUN, HUMOR, JOY, CELEBRATION

COMMUNITY
COLLABORATION, INCLUSION, BELONGING, CONSIDERATION, RESPECT

CREATIVITY
INSPIRATION, STIMULATION, PRESENCE

AUTONOMY
FULFILLING DREAMS, CHOICE, FREEDOM, SPACE, ACCEPTANCE, SELF-CARE

PURPOSE
MEANING, CONTRIBUTION, INTEGRITY, CLARITY, PERSPECTIVE

BEAUTY
HARMONY, PEACE OF MIND, ORDER, MOURNING, FAITH, HOPE, BALANCE

FEELINGS FROM MET NEEDS

HAPPY
GLAD, JOYFUL, THRILLED, CHEERFUL, UPBEAT, ECSTATIC, DELIGHTED, GIDDY

EXCITED
SURPRISED, ENERGETIC, PASSIONATE, LIVELY, AMAZED

ENGAGED
INVOLVED, FOCUSED, LIVELY, OPEN, STIMULATED, INTERESTED, ABSORBED

CONFIDENT
HOPEFUL, JAZZED, ENCOURAGED

CALM
PEACEFUL, MELLOW, SATISFIED, RELAXED, RELIEVED, OKAY, QUIET, CHILL, CENTERED, AT EASE

GRATEFUL
APPRECIATIVE, THANKFUL, TOUCHED, MOVED

LOVING
COMPASSIONATE, KIND, WARM, TENDER, OPENHEARTED

FEELINGS FROM UNMET NEEDS

SAD
UNHAPPY, BLUE, AWFUL, LOW, LONELY, BUMMED OUT

UPSET
GLOOMY, MISERABLE, MOODY, OUT OF SORTS, DISTURBED, BOTHERED, UNEASY, TROUBLED

TENSE
JITTERY, PARALYZED, FRUSTRATED, EDGY, STRESSED OUT, ANXIOUS, CLOSED, AGITATED

TIRED
BEAT, BURNED OUT, WIPED OUT, WORN OUT, POOPED, EXHAUSTED, DEPLETED, SLEEPY

MAD
ANGRY, CRANKY, FURIOUS, ANNOYED, BOTHERED, IRRITATED, AGGRAVATED, PISSED OFF

BORED
DISCONNECTED, NUMB, INDIFFERENT, WITHDRAWN, DETACHED, APATHETIC

SCARED
FEARFUL, FRIGHTENED, AFRAID, TERRIFIED, WORRIED, NERVOUS

EMBARRASSED
ASHAMED, FLUSTERED, SELF-CONSCIOUS, UNEASY, MORTIFIED

CONFUSED
UNSURE, MIXED UP, BAFFLED, PUZZLED, CONFLICTED

©2019 Amy Fabrikant & Kirsten Henning
With gratitude to Manfred Max-Neef's
Need Assessment and Maslow's Hierarchy of Needs

Learn more at AmyFabrikant.com
and KirstenHenning.com

What is Paloma feeling?

Adults who have acquired knowledge through the times and experiences they've shared with children.

DOCTOR'S NOTE ON ACTIVE LISTENING

by Dr. Emma Forbes-Jones, Clinical Psychologist

http://www.forbesjones.com/

Dr. Emma values human connection and social emotional skill building as the greatest gift we can offer young people. Emma suggests practicing Active Listening and Validation.

For some, Active Listening (AL) sounds unfamiliar and complicated, but Emma encourages everyone to try it. AL is about spending time together, being present, and connecting. It's not complicated, just the opposite. AL reduces the clutter and noise for the time spent practicing.

The key to Active Listening is not responding to what is said, and instead, offering non-verbal cues to show deep listening. The "not responding" is essential so that young person can share their feelings freely. Emma suggests practicing AL regularly to build the muscle. It works well for many as a mealtime ritual or when electronic devices, such as cell phones, tablets, video games, etc... are away for a time. For some, a car ride works well.

Caregivers can use many strategies to practice listening and validation. Emma suggests using the metaphor of sharing "A Rose and A Thorn" to create an opportunity to normalize sharing both comfortable and uncomfortable feelings on a daily basis. The rose in your day represents something that felt comfortable. The thorn in your day represents something that felt uncomfortable.

How to play ROSE AND THORN active listening:

- **One person speaks and other(s) listen.**
- **No one responds/ No follow up questions.**
- **Speaker shares their "Rose" of the day.**
- **Same speaker shares a "Thorn" of the day.**
- **Listeners may nod and follow up at a later time.***
- **When the speaker is finished, others thank the speaker for sharing.**
- **Next person shares their Rose and Thorn.**

Sometimes adults/caregivers become activated when they hear what the young people in their care have going on in their lives.

TALKING ABOUT UNCOMFORTABLE FEELINGS

Emma encourages adults to stick with the practice of listening and not responding, even if it doesn't feel like the activity is "working" or if it feels uncomfortable to hear what our young people share. Emma encourages people to think of feelings as comfortable or uncomfortable, not good or bad.

WHEN TO HAVE A FOLLOW UP CONVERSATION

Emma suggests waiting at least 30 minutes or more if possible to follow up on uncomfortable Rose & Thorn shares. It is often best if you are able to take time to process and receive some support or guidance around the concern.

WHERE TO HAVE THE FOLLOW UP CONVERSATION

When choosing the time to follow up on the Rose & Thorn share, look for a moment when the child is not engaged in another activity. We don't want to make them feel uncomfortable or "punished" for sharing honestly with us.

Emma suggests asking the child, "Is this a good time for us to talk about....." If the child says not now, then ask, "Okay, if now is not good for you, when are we going to have this conversation?"

Things to keep in mind when you feel scared for the child:

- We don't have to "fix" it

- Be responsive, not responsible

- Children want to be heard

- Children are not responsible to carry the weight of the caregiver. They need love and support, especially when they are sending out fear and grief (see 3 concentric circles of childcare on the next page).

- We can help children get the support they need to work it out (call pediatrician, therapist, teacher, etc...)

- Adults often need to receive support BEFORE they interact with the child

- Create an adult support network from other adults (friends, family, support group, mental health professional, etc....)

RECOMMENDED RESOURCES

Anxiety and Depression Association of America
http://www.adaa.org

American Academy of Child and Adolescent Psychiatry
http://www.aacap.org

American Psychiatric Association
http://www.psychiatry.org

American Psychological Association
http://www.apa.org

The Depressed Child Resources
http://www.depressedchild.org/Resources/resources.htm

Healthy Children
https://www.healthychildren.org

KidsHealth
www.kidshealth.org

NAMI, National Alliance on Mental Illness
https://www.nami.org/

Made in the USA
Middletown, DE
11 May 2019